THE PUPPY PLACE

JACK

THE PUPPY PLACE

THE PUPPY PLACE

JACK

ELLEN MILES

LITTLE APPLE

SCHOLASTIC INC.

New York   Toronto   London   Auckland
Sydney   Mexico City   New Delhi   Hong Kong

ISBN-13: 978-0-545-16810-6
ISBN-10: 0-545-16810-4

Cover art by Tim O'Brien
Original cover design by Steve Scott

12 11 10 9 8 7 6 5   10 11 12 13 14/0

Printed in the U.S.A.

First printing, October 2009

For Beverly Cleary, with admiration and gratitude

CHAPTER ONE

Dear Kit Smithers,

My name is Lizzie Peterson, and I am in fourth grade. I am writing to you because you are my favorite author. Your books are the best. I have read almost all of them exsept *Islanders*, but my favorite one is *Mountain Girl*. It's so exciting. My favorite part is when Sunny thinks she hears a bear in the woods.

I can tell that you like dogs because you put dogs in all your books and they always seem like real dogs, not book dogs, if you know what I mean. I love dogs, espeshally puppies. I have a puppy named Buddy. He is the cutest. My family even fosters puppies. That means we take care of puppies who need homes, just until we can find each one the perfect forever family.

My family is:

— my dad, who is a firefighter
— my mom, who is a writter like you, only she's a newspaper reporter
— my younger brother Charles (annoying)
— my youngest brother, the Bean (real name: Adam) (also annoying).

Lizzie leaned back from the computer to read over what she had written so far. Was it getting too long? No, it was good. Even Charles would probably say so. Charles was always writing letters. One of them, about a beagle puppy who was not being treated well, had even gotten published in the newspaper. But so far, letters had not really been Lizzie's thing.

Lizzie's thing was reading. Lately it seemed like all she wanted to do was read, read, read.

(And play with dogs and puppies, of course. That would always be her first choice.) And she especially loved reading Kit Smithers's books. Kit Smithers wrote stories about girls Lizzie's age who did cool things, like paddling canoes or surviving in the wilderness by eating roots and berries.

After she had read all six of the Kit Smithers books at the library, Lizzie had begged her mom to buy her three more, including a hardcover copy of *Mountain Girl* with beautiful illustrations. She'd gobbled those books up, too, and then started all over again. Finally, one Friday night after supper, she'd decided she just had to let Kit Smithers know how much she, Lizzie Peterson, loved her books.

Now Lizzie looked at the screen and started to write again.

I don't have a real job, since I'm only in fourth grade, but I volonteere at the animal shelter every single Saturday, and sometimes I help out at my aunt Amanda's doggy day care. One day she had 37 dogs to take care of! I am very good at training dogs. I trained our puppy, Buddy, to sit, stay, come, sit up pretty (like, sitting with his front paws held up), shake, and fetch. Only, when he fetches, he doesn't always bring the ball back and you have to chase him for it, which he thinks is a game, so he runs even faster. Buddy is brown with a white spot on his chest in the shape of a heart. He is a good boy and I love him.

Lizzie looked down at the floor, where Buddy was snoozing, curled up in a snug ball. First his nose and then his paws began to twitch, and Buddy let out a little snuffly half bark. Lizzie's dad said that meant a dog was dreaming. Lizzie liked to imagine what Buddy might be dreaming about. Treats, probably. He sure did love those new biscuits Mom had bought, the ones that looked like tiny lamb chops. Or maybe he was dreaming about chasing squirrels. Buddy loved to tear after the squirrels in the backyard, even though he never came close to catching one.

Lizzie wanted to pick Buddy up and hug him and kiss his soft puppy fur and stroke his silky ears. But he looked so content, asleep on the thick rug. She decided to wait. Maybe he would wake up by the time she was done with her letter.

Lizzie planned to draw some pictures on the letter after she printed it out. Maybe a horse, which she had just learned to draw. Her best friend, Maria, had taught her. Maria really loved horses, and she could draw them so they looked 100 percent real. So far Lizzie's horses looked sort of like sock puppets, but she just needed more practice.

Lizzie finished the letter.

Please write back as soon as you can.
Yours sinserely, Lizzie Peterson, your #1 fan

She did spell-check and found a few mistakes, which she corrected. Then she printed out the letter. It filled a whole page! There wasn't much room for horse drawings, so she drew dog paw prints and flowers all around the edges, using every color of marker she had. At the bottom, near where she signed her name, Lizzie drew a picture of Sunny, the main character in *Mountain Girl*. It came out so well she almost wanted to keep it, but then she thought of how impressed Kit Smithers would be.

She found an envelope in a drawer and wrote *Kit Smithers, author* on it. Then Lizzie realized that she did not know Kit Smithers's address.

When she stood up, Buddy jumped up, too. His tail wagged, his eyes shone, and his ears were all perky. What a happy dog. Lizzie loved that about Buddy. He was always excited to see what would happen next. "We're only going down to Mom's study, that's all," she told him. Buddy didn't care.

It was still an adventure. He charged down the hall in front of her.

Mom liked to work on her newspaper articles in the evening, while Lizzie and Charles did their homework and the Bean was in bed. Right now Mom was writing a long article about a man who ran a green building business. She had talked about it at dinner the night before. At first Lizzie and Charles had both thought that meant that the man built greenhouses. Or green houses. But it turned out to mean that he built houses that did not use as much energy as regular houses. Lizzie paused in the doorway to watch Mom tap away on her computer. How could anybody type so fast?

"Mom?"

Mom spun around on her chair and smiled at Lizzie. "Hi, sweetie! What have you got there?"

Lizzie held up the envelope. "I wrote a letter to Kit Smithers, but I don't know her address."

"I bet she'll love getting a letter from you." Mom

leaned back and stretched. "Bring me one of her books and we'll see who the publisher is. We can send your letter to her publisher, and they'll send it on to her."

Lizzie ran to her room and found one of her other Kit Smithers favorites, *The Long Valley*, on her bookshelf. When she brought it back, Mom showed her the name and address of Kit Smithers's publisher, right on one of the front pages. Lizzie was copying it onto the envelope when the phone rang.

Mom picked it up. "Hello? Oh, hello, Amanda. How are you?" She listened.

Lizzie waved. "Tell Aunt Amanda I said hi!"

Mom held up a finger. "What's that? You have a puppy you want us to foster?"

Lizzie stopped writing. "A puppy? What kind? Where did it come from? Can we foster it? Please? Please?"

Mom frowned at Lizzie and made a "zip-the-lip" motion. "Tonight? Amanda, are you serious?"

Lizzie jumped up and down. "Say yes! Say yes! I'll do all the work, I promise! A new puppy! Yay!"

Mom sighed. "Okay, Amanda. I guess if you're that desperate, we can help you out. But only for tonight."

CHAPTER TWO

"What kind of puppy? How old? Boy or girl? Why does it need a new home?" Lizzie peppered her mother with questions.

"Lizzie, Lizzie. Easy, there! I don't know the answers to any of those questions, but we'll both know soon. Aunt Amanda is on her way over right now. All she said was to get the crate ready, and to make sure Buddy is shut up in your room —"

"What? Why does Buddy have to get shut up in Lizzie's room? And did I hear something about a puppy?" Charles appeared in the doorway. Buddy ran over to greet him.

"We're getting a new foster puppy!" Lizzie couldn't wait to tell her brother the news.

"We're not necessarily fostering the puppy," Mom told Charles. "Your aunt Amanda's in a pinch because she has a homeless puppy on her hands and an obedience class to teach tonight. And as for Buddy, he only has to be shut up for a little while, when the new puppy first comes over."

"Did you hear that, Buddy?" Charles bent down to pat Buddy. "It's only for a little while. And we'll still always love you best, no matter what."

Buddy wagged his tail and licked Charles's hand.

I know you love me! I love you, too.

Charles hugged Buddy. Then he and Lizzie walked their puppy down the hall and got him settled in Lizzie's room. "He'll be happy in here with his favorite toy." Lizzie tucked Mr. Duck between Buddy's paws.

"He likes Pooh better." Charles offered a stuffed

bear to Buddy. Buddy grabbed Pooh happily and thumped his tail, leaving Mr. Duck facedown and forgotten.

"Told you so," said Charles.

Lizzie gritted her teeth. Charles had really been bugging her lately. What a pest! But she had better things to think about: a new foster pup was going to arrive any minute. She gave Buddy a bedtime snack of two of the little lamb-chop biscuits. Then she and Charles went downstairs to find Mom and Dad in the kitchen, setting up the puppy crate. Lizzie had brought down her letter to Kit Smithers. She leaned it against the salt-shaker on the kitchen table so she'd see it the next morning and wouldn't forget to mail it.

The very first time she had seen a puppy crate, Lizzie had thought it looked like a cage. She had thought it would be mean to keep a dog in such a small space. But by now, after her family had fostered so many puppies, she knew better. Lizzie knew that a crate was a great way to give a puppy a place of its own, like a little cave where it felt safe and sound. She knew that a crate could help with house-training, since most puppies didn't like to go to the bathroom where they slept, and that it could help with bad habits like chewing, because if a puppy was shut up inside his crate, he couldn't get into tempting things like old shoes or the garbage.

Lizzie went to the hall closet to find the red flannel sheet the Petersons had used over and over again with different puppies they had fostered. She held it to her nose and took a big sniff. Even though they washed it between puppies, it always had that special, delicious puppy smell. She brought the soft old sheet to the kitchen and folded it up so it made a cozy bed inside the crate.

Charles had gone into the living room to round up a few puppy toys, and he tucked them inside the crate, too. Mom got out the dishes they used for foster puppies, and Dad filled the water bowl.

"What a team!" he said as he looked around the kitchen. "I think we're all ready."

As if Aunt Amanda had heard him, there was a knock at the back door, and she burst in, towed by a sleek, muscular brown puppy with a pure white bib and paws and a funny, squashed black face framed by floppy ears. His big brown eyes shone. He wagged his short stubby tail as he pulled the leash right out of Aunt Amanda's hands and danced and pranced his way around the kitchen, greeting each of the Petersons in turn.

"Look at him! He's all muscle. What a little tank," said Dad.

"Jack! Slow down, buddy!" Aunt Amanda sounded exasperated, but she was laughing, too. Lizzie could see that it was hard not to laugh around this puppy. What a clown! He snuffled and sniffed at everything, reminding Lizzie of Pugsley, a naughty little pug the Petersons had fostered. But this dog was much bigger than a pug and had longer legs.

"Hello, Jack." Lizzie squatted down to pet him. The puppy snorted happily and licked her face all over.

Hi! Hi! Hello! What fun to meet somebody new!

"Is he a boxer?" Lizzie asked Aunt Amanda.

Her aunt smiled and nodded. "Good guess."

It wasn't exactly a guess. Lizzie had practically memorized the "Dog Breeds of the World" poster in her room. But even though she knew what boxers looked like, she had never met one before. Jack was adorable! And he sure was a ball of energy.

"How old is he?" Charles sat down on the floor next to Lizzie so he could get his own face licked.

"Jack is about nine months old." Aunt Amanda laughed as she watched the puppy climb all over Lizzie and Charles. "And he's really a very good boy. Except . . ."

"Except?" Mom asked.

"Maybe it's time for you to tell us why he needs a new home." Dad raised an eyebrow at his sister.

Aunt Amanda checked her watch, then started speaking quickly. "It's sort of sad. Jack just started coming to Bowser's Backyard last week. I had a funny feeling about his owners. They seemed almost out of patience with Jack. They brought him to doggy day care every single day, even on the weekend, when they weren't at work, and they were often late to pick him up. It was almost as if they wished they'd never gotten a dog. And sure enough, they just plain did not come to pick him up tonight. When I tried to call them, their phone had been disconnected. I drove by their house, but there were no lights on and there was a SOLD sign on the front lawn. I think they moved away and left Jack behind. They gave up on this boy."

Jack tugged at Lizzie's shoelaces, snuffling and grunting as he did his best to pull them right out of her sneakers. Lizzie felt so sorry for the puppy. "How could anybody abandon you like that?" She pulled him into her arms for a hug. At first he wriggled and squirmed, trying to lick her nose and ears and chin. Then, as she patted him, he calmed down and snuggled in next to her with his head on her lap. He gazed up at her, wrinkling his forehead in a very worried way. His sad little face melted Lizzie's heart.

Will you be my friend? Everybody else is always mad at me. They yell and yell. I need a friend.

"Aww, Jack. It's all going to be okay." Lizzie patted him some more. With one long sigh, Jack closed his eyes and fell asleep. Lizzie could tell that it had been a long day for the little pup.

Mom looked at Aunt Amanda. "So, what was the problem? Why were Jack's owners out of patience?"

"I'll explain it all tomorrow." Aunt Amanda checked her watch again. "But I can't stay another second. I'm already ten minutes late for obedience class and my students are waiting. Just make sure to keep an eye on Jack all the time. He should definitely sleep inside his crate tonight, too. I can't thank you enough for helping me out!" With a quick kiss on Jack's nose and a wave, Aunt Amanda was gone.

CHAPTER THREE

"You're going to love Jack," Lizzie told Buddy as she got ready for bed that night. "You'll meet him in the morning, and I bet you'll be friends right away."

Buddy cocked his head and gave Lizzie a questioning look.

I smell a new puppy in the house. Do you like him better than me?

Lizzie went over to pat Buddy, who was curled up on the foot of her bed. "You know you'll always be my favorite dog in the world, right?" She lay down next to him and kissed his darling little black nose. "You really are my best buddy. And you're always so nice to the other puppies we foster. You get along with everybody!"

Buddy nuzzled Lizzie's ear and licked her cheek. She could smell his sweet puppy breath. Then he closed his eyes and went back to sleep. Lizzie watched Buddy for a moment. Was there ever a cuter puppy? He was such a good boy, too. He had been shut up in her room all evening, except for when she'd taken him out for a pee, and he'd never complained once.

Lizzie climbed into bed and pulled up the covers. Good thing the next day was Saturday! Except for a couple of hours when she would be volunteering at the animal shelter, she would have most of the day to get to know Jack and help him get settled. She had a good feeling about the little boxer puppy. Jack was all safe and sound in his crate down in the kitchen, where he couldn't get into any trouble. Lizzie yawned, stretched, and turned over in her comfy bed. She was so sleepy.

Bang!

Bang! Bang! Bang!

Lizzie woke up suddenly. What was that sound coming from downstairs?

"OoooOOOOoooooOOOO!"

And what was *that* sound?

Buddy jumped off the bed and ran to the door. "OOOOooooOOOO!" he howled along with the sound from downstairs.

"Oh, no!" Lizzie threw back the covers and jumped out of bed. Those sounds had to be Jack howling and banging on his crate. "You stay here, Buddy." Lizzie put on her bathrobe and shuffled into her slippers, then headed down the dark stairs. Lizzie had heard puppies whimper and cry before, but this was something else. Why was the puppy making so much noise in the middle of the night?

By the time Lizzie turned on the kitchen light, Jack had stopped howling and banging. He sat in his crate, looking sadly back at Lizzie. He blinked his big brown eyes.

"Awww." Lizzie sat down on the floor next to the crate and opened the door. Jack ran right out. He squirmed onto her lap and licked her chin.

I hate it in there! I'm bored and lonely!

"Poor little guy." Lizzie patted Jack. His fur was so short and his little body was so muscular! He wasn't like any of the pudgy puppies she had taken care of before. Lizzie noticed that the two puppy toys Charles had left in the crate were shredded into little pieces. Oops. Oh, well. You had to expect that puppy toys wouldn't last forever. She started to pick up the furry shreds.

"I guess our new friend doesn't like his crate." Dad stood in the kitchen doorway, yawning and rubbing his eyes. He must have heard all the noise, too. Mom, Charles, and the Bean could sleep through a parade *and* fireworks, but Lizzie and Dad were light sleepers and woke up easily.

"I guess not. Maybe he's just too excited about being in a new place." Lizzie stuffed the shredded toys into her bathrobe pocket. She patted Jack some more as he snorted and snuffled happily.

"I suppose." Dad looked tired. "Well, let's try to get him settled again, and see how he does."

Lizzie used a biscuit to tempt Jack back into the crate. She patted him and talked to him in a soft, low voice until he looked sleepy and relaxed. "Okay, little Jackie. You sleep well now," she said as she and Dad turned off the light and tip-toed away.

Back upstairs, Lizzie had just drifted off to sleep when the banging started all over again. *Bang! Bang!* Lizzie put her pillow over her head to block out the sound.

"OOOOooooOOOOOoooo!" Jack began to howl.

"OooOOOOOoooOOOOO!" Buddy howled back.

Lizzie sighed and took the pillow off her head. She got out of bed, put her robe and slippers back on, and went downstairs. "What's the matter, Jack?" The puppy sat in his cage, holding up one paw. He looked extra cute and extra sad. "Awww, poor thing."

"Maybe he's just doing it to get attention." Dad had come downstairs again, too.

Lizzie nodded. "Remember Pugsley?" she asked. "He needed attention. And when he got it, he was a much better puppy." She let Jack out of his crate and patted him for a long time.

Dad sat down on the floor and patted Jack, too. "But we can't stay up with him all night," he said after a while. "Jack seems happier now. Let's try putting him back to bed in his crate."

This time, they had barely made it to the bottom of the stairs before the howling began. "OOOOOOoooooOOOOOO!" *Bang! Bang! Bang!*

Lizzie and Dad looked at each other and shrugged. Then they turned around and went back. Lizzie checked out the kitchen. The garbage was under the sink, safe behind the cabinet doors. The counters were high. There was no food on the table. "He can't really get into any trouble in here," she said. "What if we just use the baby gate to keep him in the kitchen? Maybe he'll be happier if he's not locked in the crate."

"That sounds like an excellent idea." Dad set up the baby gate, and Lizzie opened the door of the crate and left it open so that Jack could still use the soft sheet inside for a bed if he wanted. Jack watched them leave the kitchen, but he did not howl. They made it all the way upstairs. Still no howling! Dad looked at Lizzie and smiled. "I think he's okay now," he said as he kissed her good night for the third time.

Lizzie went back to bed and didn't wake up until early the next morning, when she heard Mom shout, "Oh, no! Look what this puppy has done!"

CHAPTER FOUR

Mom groaned so loudly that Lizzie could hear her all the way upstairs. "Oh, what a mess!" Then Lizzie heard Mom begin to lecture the puppy. "You are a very, very, *very* bad —"

"Wait!" Lizzie jumped out of bed and ran to the top of the stairs. "Don't yell at him! Don't punish him!" She did not even know for sure exactly what the new puppy had done to make Mom so upset, but she did know one thing: there was no use in yelling at or punishing a puppy for something he had already done. Unless you caught a puppy in the middle of chewing your shoe, or peeing on the living room carpet, it was too late. If you yelled at him afterward, he wouldn't understand why you were mad. Aunt Amanda had explained all that to Lizzie, and it made sense. Puppies had to learn what was right and wrong, and the best way to teach them was to make a fuss over them when they did something right, like going to the bathroom outside, and ignore them when they did something wrong, like eating your favorite socks.

Lizzie ran down to the kitchen. Dad and Charles and the Bean thundered down the stairs behind her. The four of them stood at the kitchen door and stared at the mess Jack had made.

"Uh-oh," said the Bean.

"Wow!" said Charles.

"Yikes!" said Lizzie.

Dad didn't say a word. He just burst out laughing.

"It's not funny!" Mom stood in the middle of the kitchen, hands on her hips. She glared at Jack, who sat near her feet. The puppy cocked his head and gave his tail the tiniest wag as he greeted the newcomers.

Hi there! See what I did? I was so bored, but I found a way to have fun.

Mom and Jack were surrounded by a sea of shredded paper, scraps of milk carton and foil, orange peels, coffee grounds, apple cores, the take-out containers from last night's Chinese dinner, and the remains of the plastic pumpkins Charles and the Bean had used for trick-or-treating. It was the middle of November, but they still had a little candy left from Halloween.

"Uh-oh," the Bean said again.

"My candy!" Charles wailed. "I thought it would be safe up on the counter."

"Was there any chocolate in there?" Lizzie grabbed Charles's arm.

"Ow, no!" He rubbed his arm and glared at her. "I ate it all the first week. The Bean ate his, too."

"That's all right, then," said Lizzie. "At least there wasn't any chocolate left. Chocolate can be very bad for dogs. It can make them really sick."

Personally, she always kept her candy on the top shelf of her closet, in her room. It was safer there. She looked around at the mess and tried to think of something positive to say. "What a smartie! Jack figured out how to get into the garbage and up onto the counters."

"Lizzie!" For some reason, this made Mom even madder. "And, you, stop laughing." She glared at Dad, who was still chuckling.

"At least he doesn't seem to have gotten sick from it all." Dad was obviously trying to see the bright side, too.

Lizzie had just stepped over the baby gate to help clean up when she saw that Jack had stopped wagging his tail. His ears perked up and the fur rose on the back of his thick, muscular neck. He growled, and Lizzie saw his lip curl, showing his teeth.

"Uh-oh," said the Bean.

Lizzie turned to see Buddy standing near Charles on the other side of the baby gate. In her rush to get downstairs, she'd forgotten to close her bedroom door. Buddy had followed her. "Charles! Grab Buddy and take him outside!"

Charles made a face. "Who made you the boss?"

"I remember reading that some boxers have trouble getting along with other dogs," Lizzie told him. "We don't want them to fight, do we?"

"Fine!" said Charles. "But if I do it, you better give me some of your leftover candy."

"Why should I?" she asked. "Just because I was smart enough to put mine in a safe place —"

"Candy!" the Bean wailed. "My candy all gone?" The terrible truth had finally sunk in.

"Now look what you've done." Dad frowned at Lizzie.

Mom frowned at Dad. "It's not her fault. It's the puppy's."

"Don't blame Jack!" Charles frowned at Mom.

"Uh-oh." The Bean started to wail even more loudly.

Buddy looked from one face to another and began to whimper.

Why is everybody so mad? Did I do something wrong?

"Oh, Buddy! It's okay!" Lizzie couldn't blame Buddy for crying. She felt like crying, too. Jack looked up at her with his big brown eyes. His tail drooped, his ears were back, and his rear legs trembled. Lizzie knew that meant he was scared and upset. "Wait, everybody!" She dropped to her knees and began to pet Jack. "We have to stop arguing. We're all upset, and now Jack and Buddy are upset, too."

"But —" Charles began.

"Lizzie is right," interrupted Dad. "Charles, why don't you take Buddy outside? I'll take the Bean upstairs and get him dressed."

"And Lizzie and I will clean up," Mom said.

31

"Then maybe we can start this day all over again." She smiled at Dad.

Lizzie felt better — so much better that she turned to face Charles. "And I'll give you and the Bean some of my candy," she said. It wasn't a big sacrifice, since she was sick of SweeTarts and Life Savers, the only candy she had left. But the offer made Charles smile.

Lizzie petted Jack's head as they watched Charles and Buddy go outside. "It's okay. I bet anything that you'll be friends when you get to know each other." Jack snuffled, put his paws up on Lizzie's leg, and gazed at her with his big brown eyes.

Are you mad at me? I think the other person is upset with me.

"It's okay," Lizzie told the puppy again as she began to help Mom pick up the garbage. Then she spotted something lying on the floor. A crumpled envelope and a torn, stained sheet of paper — with brightly colored drawings all over it. "Oh, no," she said. "My letter to Kit Smithers!" She turned to face Jack. "You are a very, *very* bad —"

CHAPTER FIVE

"Lizzie! Wait!" Mom stopped Lizzie just in time, before she yelled at the puppy. "Remember what you said? He doesn't understand what he did wrong."

"But my letter!" Lizzie held up the torn, crumpled scraps. "I worked so hard on that picture of Sunny!" She let her arm drop to her side. Mom was right. It wasn't fair to yell at Jack. But boy, was she mad.

Mom took the letter and smoothed it out on the kitchen table. "I wonder if we used some tape . . . No, it's really too far gone." She turned to Lizzie. "That really was a nice picture you drew," she said. "I can see that. But you'll just have to print the letter out again and draw some more pictures."

"I don't have time! I'm supposed to be at the shelter by noon." Lizzie had not missed a single Saturday volunteering at the animal shelter, and she wasn't about to start now. She crossed her arms and glared at Jack. Lizzie had really, really wanted that letter to be on its way to Kit Smithers by today. She couldn't wait to hear back from her favorite author. Maybe she was acting babyish, but she couldn't help it.

"I'll tell you what," said Mom. "You have the letter on the computer, right? How about if we do some research together and see if we can find an e-mail address to send it to? That would be faster than the regular mail anyway."

Lizzie thought about this. "But what about my drawings?"

"I can attach a picture of you with Buddy instead. Kit Smithers would probably enjoy seeing what you look like." Mom put a hand on Lizzie's shoulder. "I know you're disappointed, but it's not the end of the world."

Easy for Mom to say. Lizzie looked down at Jack. He gazed back at her with his big brown eyes. Who would imagine that such a sweet, innocent little puppy could be so naughty? "I know it's not your fault, Jack." Lizzie bent to pet him. "But please, please, can't you try to be a good boy and stop eating things?"

When Charles came back inside with Buddy, Lizzie took Jack outside so Buddy could eat his breakfast in peace. "Bring Buddy out when he's done, and we can give them a chance to get to know each other," she told Charles. Lizzie knew that having lots of space to run around would be a good thing if the puppies didn't get along right away. On her way out, she grabbed her copy of *Mountain Girl* from the shelf in the living room so she could read while the puppies played.

When Charles brought Buddy out, Jack didn't growl even once. Instead, he bowed down and wagged his tail, inviting Buddy to play. "Maybe he only growled before because he felt like the kitchen was his territory," Lizzie said. Soon both puppies zoomed crazily around the yard, chasing each other through the piles of leaves that had fallen from the trees.

Charles sat down next to Lizzie on the deck and they laughed as they watched the puppies play. Then Charles showed Lizzie a crumpled piece of paper. "I found your letter in the kitchen. Too bad Jack ate it."

Lizzie nodded. "I know. You should have seen how good my picture was."

"I guess he ate the part where you asked her some questions." Charles raised his eyebrows.

Lizzie grabbed the letter. "What do you mean?"

"I mean, it's a good letter and everything," Charles said. "But when Mr. Mason taught us about letters, he said you should always ask the person some questions, and I don't see any here." He held up his hands. "Just an idea."

"Hmph." Lizzie crossed her arms over her chest. When had her little brother become such a know-it-all? True, he had written to three authors in the past year and he had gotten letters back from all of them. One of them had even sent a signed picture of himself. But Lizzie knew perfectly well how to write letters.

The puppies were still zooming around the yard. Now Buddy was showing Jack how to play tug with a stick. When Jack managed to grab the stick away, he carried it proudly back to Lizzie. "Good boy, Jack!" she said as she petted him.

Yay! I guess I did something right for a change!

Mom opened the back door. "Lizzie, Charles! Aunt Amanda's here to tell us more about Jack. Bring the puppies inside."

"I am so sorry," Aunt Amanda was saying when Lizzie and Charles went into the kitchen. Mom must have already told her how Jack had destroyed the entire kitchen. Lizzie got Jack a treat and sat down on the floor with the puppy on her lap.

Mom looked at Aunt Amanda. "So, was this the problem? Was this kind of behavior why Jack's owners were out of patience?"

"Well . . ." Aunt Amanda looked down at the floor and kicked one foot into the other. She looked just like Charles did when he got caught tracking mud into the living room. "Yes. That's the problem. Jack eats things."

"What's the big deal?" asked Lizzie. "All puppies chew."

Aunt Amanda sighed. "Not like this puppy."

CHAPTER SIX

There was a knock at the door, and Aunt Amanda looked relieved. "Whew. Perfect timing. That's probably my friend Eileen. I asked her to come over to help me explain about Jack." Aunt Amanda opened the door. Eileen was very short, with wild curly hair and rosy cheeks. Lizzie thought she had seen her somewhere before.

"You look familiar," Eileen said to Lizzie after Aunt Amanda had introduced everyone. Then she snapped her fingers. "I met you at the Halloween party! You were dressed as Scooby-Doo, right?"

Lizzie smiled and put on her Scooby voice. "Ruh-roh!" So that was where she had seen this woman. "Now I remember you, too. You were Little Bo

Peep." Aunt Amanda's Halloween party had been a blast. All the doggy day care clients had dressed up their dogs for a costume contest. There were cowboy dogs and Star Wars dogs and ghost dogs. One lady had even dressed her dog up as a cat and won second prize! First prize had gone to Hoss, the big Great Dane, who had come as an elephant. They'd had games (Dunking for Doggy Biscuits, Chase the Ghost, Fetch the Stuffed Bat) and treats (pumpkin-shaped cookies), and they'd even done a craft project (paw-print holiday cards).

"That's right!" Aunt Amanda nodded. "Eileen was at the party. She just moved into the office next door. Eileen is an animal behaviorist."

"A what?" Charles stared at Eileen.

Eileen laughed. "Not many people have heard of my job. What I do is study how animals act. Some behaviorists study wild animals, but I mostly study pets. I help people understand why their dogs and cats, and even their horses, behave the way they do. I can help if you have a pet with a problem, like fighting with other animals, or running away, or" — she cleared her throat and looked at Jack, who had fallen asleep and was snoring gently on Lizzie's lap — "chewing and eating things he shouldn't. . . ."

"Eileen helps owners figure out how to help their animals learn to behave better, so they don't have to give them away, or abandon them like Jack's owners did," Aunt Amanda finished for her friend. "She is a wizard with animals."

Eileen ducked her head, and her cheeks turned even rosier. "I don't know about that, but I do love working with them." She came over to pet Jack. "I've heard some stories about this little guy." She shook her head.

"Such as?" Mom folded her arms across her chest.

Lizzie crossed her fingers and hoped Eileen wouldn't say something really awful about Jack's behavior. She was already in love with the wacky pup who was fast asleep in her lap, and she hoped like anything that the Petersons would get to foster him, no matter how much trouble he was. They had taken care of naughty puppies before. They could handle a dog who chewed a little.

"Well" — Eileen exchanged a glance with Aunt Amanda — "like most boxers, he has a lot of energy and he's very curious. He can be, um, kind of destructive. According to his owners, he has chewed and even eaten up some really weird things."

"Like what?" Now Dad looked worried.

"A cell phone," said Aunt Amanda. "And soap. And money, and marshmallows, and a whole bag of cookies — plus the bag itself."

"And three pencils and some sand and a birthday cake and . . . rocks." Eileen's eyes were bright and Lizzie thought she was trying not to smile. "It's pretty amazing, really. Jack has eaten just about everything you can think of."

"Doesn't he get a bellyache?" Charles stared at Jack.

Aunt Amanda nodded. "Jack has made himself very, very sick. He's been to the vet many times in the last month. And even though he's only nine months old, he's already had three operations. I think that's partly why my clients gave him up. They just couldn't afford the vet bills anymore."

"Plus, they both have busy jobs, and not enough time to give Jack the attention he needs," Eileen said. "I had just started to work with them on his behavior, but I think they were shocked when they understood how much time and energy it might take to teach Jack not to chew and eat things."

Lizzie looked down at Jack. He looked so innocent, lying there with his head on her knee. How could his owners have given up on him? "We'll find Jack the perfect home," she said. She looked up in time to see Mom and Dad glance at each other.

"I only agreed to take him for one night," Mom said.

"But he needs us!" Lizzie stroked Jack's head.

"Lizzie, I don't know," Dad began. "This dog may need more attention than we can give him."

"I'll help," Charles said. "I promise."

Mom sighed. "I know you both want to help Jack. I do, too. But I'm not sure we can handle him."

"I can give you some good advice if you agree to foster Jack," Eileen offered. "No charge."

Lizzie gave Eileen a grateful smile.

"How about this?" Dad asked. "Let's agree to keep him for the rest of the weekend and see how it goes. After that, we'll have to see."

Mom nodded. "That sounds like a good plan."

"Yay!" yelled Lizzie and Charles.

Jack woke up. He jumped to his feet and began to spin around in circles, dancing happily.

Aunt Amanda smiled. "I don't think you'll be sorry," she said.

Mom shook her head. "I hope you're right."

After Aunt Amanda and Eileen left, Lizzie and Charles took the puppies back outside. "We'd better keep a really close eye on Jack today, and make sure he gets plenty of playtime," Lizzie told her brother. "If he keeps chewing things up and keeping us awake at night, Mom and Dad won't let us foster him."

Charles nodded. "Good plan."

They took turns all morning. Lizzie watched the puppies while Charles went to soccer practice; then he watched them while she went to volunteer at the animal shelter. When she got back home from Caring Paws, Lizzie was tired. She had walked six dogs, cleaned out three kennels, and fed sixteen cats. But she played fetch with Jack while Charles went next door, where his best friend, Sammy, lived. When Charles came back, Lizzie went upstairs. All she really wanted to do by then was lie on her bed and read for a while, but instead she sat down at the computer and found the letter she had written to Kit Smithers. She read it over. Then she added a few sentences at the end.

We got a new foster puppy last night. His name is Jack and he is a boxer. He's very cute and smart but kind of naughty.

Oh, and I have some questions for you. How did you decide to be a writer? Are the stories you write based on true stories, or do you make them up? Do you draw the pictures in the books? Are you going to write more books? Do you have a dog? What is your favorite color?

When she was done, she went to find Mom. She was ready to e-mail her letter to Kit Smithers.

CHAPTER SEVEN

Mom was in her study. She sat at her desk, her head in her hands. Lizzie thought she looked upset.

"Did Jack eat something?" Lizzie was alarmed. Maybe Charles had not watched the puppy closely enough while Lizzie had worked on her letter.

"No, it's not that." Mom sighed and sat up, revealing a pile of papers on her desk. "It's just that I can't seem to take these notes and make them into a good newspaper article. When I interviewed this man about his green building business, I thought I understood it. But now, I keep reading through my notes, and I'm not so sure."

"That's too bad," said Lizzie. But she was relieved. At least Jack hadn't done anything else wrong. So far. "I have my letter all ready to send to Kit Smithers." She held up the flash drive she used to save all her homework and other important things.

Mom stuck the drive into her computer. "Let's see if we can find a Web site," she said. Mom typed in Kit Smithers's name. When the list of possible sites came up, Lizzie pointed to one.

"Click on that one," she said.

Mom clicked on the heading and a new page opened up.

"That's her!" Lizzie looked over her mom's shoulder. "That's Kit Smithers! That's the same picture of her that's in the back of *Mountain Girl*." Lizzie had studied that picture plenty of times, imagining how exciting it would be to visit Kit Smithers in Houston, Texas, where the caption said she lived.

"She looks like a nice person," said Mom. They

clicked around some more and found pictures of Kit Smithers as a little girl, a page with advice about writing, and a page about a brand-new book that would be coming out in a month. It was called *Northern Lights,* and as soon as Lizzie saw the sled dog team and the polar bear on the cover, she wanted that book.

"Look! There's a place you can click if you want to send her mail." Lizzie pointed.

Mom clicked, and an e-mail form popped up. She copied Lizzie's letter from the flash drive into the e-mail. Then she attached a picture of Lizzie with Buddy, the one from last Christmas with them sitting under the tree together, Buddy snoozing in Lizzie's lap.

"Put 'from your number one fan, Lizzie' in the subject line," said Lizzie, "so she knows it's from me even though it's from your e-mail account."

Mom typed that in.

Lizzie leaned over and clicked "send." She couldn't wait one minute longer. The sooner they sent the e-mail, the sooner she might hear back from Kit Smithers. That would be so cool. She imagined telling Maria. She imagined telling her whole class. Everybody would definitely be impressed. Lizzie stared at the screen, wishing a reply would appear instantly.

"Okay," Mom said. "I'd better get back to work."

That meant Lizzie was supposed to leave the study. "But you'll keep checking to see if she answered, right?"

"I'll keep checking," said Mom. "But don't be surprised if it takes longer than you think. She might be very busy."

Lizzie headed downstairs. It was her turn to watch Jack, anyway. She found Charles and the Bean outside with the puppies.

Charles waved to Lizzie. "Watch this! Jack already learned a trick!" He held a toy just above Jack's head. "Sit, Jack." Jack sat. Then Charles held the toy a little higher over Jack's head. "Now, sit pretty, Jack." Jack raised his front paws off the ground, balancing on his hind legs. He could hold the pose for only a few seconds.

The Bean loved that trick. "Again!" he shouted as soon as Jack was back on all four feet. "Again!"

"Wow." Lizzie wished she had been the one to teach Jack a trick. "He sure is a smart puppy," she said. "I just know we'll find him a great home." She ran for the camera and took a whole bunch of pictures of Jack. She took some of Buddy, too, so he wouldn't feel left out.

When the phone rang, Lizzie answered. It was Eileen. "I'm just calling to see how things are going with Jack," she said.

"Well," said Lizzie, "we're just trying to keep him busy. I was thinking I could bring his crate up to my room tonight. Maybe he'll be able to sleep inside it if he's not all alone in the kitchen."

"Great idea!" said Eileen. "That is exactly what I would have suggested. Boxers like to be close to their people. The perfect owner for Jack would be someone who works at home, so he wouldn't be left alone."

Lizzie told Eileen about how she and Charles had taken turns playing with Jack, mostly outdoors, hoping to tire him out.

"You're on the right track," said Eileen. "Jack would probably be happiest living somewhere in the country, where he could really run around."

Lizzie also told Eileen about how she had not yelled at Jack because she had not caught him in the middle of eating things.

"Excellent!" said Eileen. "And if you *do* catch him, you can try saying 'leave it,' then give him a treat when he drops whatever he's chewing. Eventually he'll learn the 'leave it' command. It sounds as if you really understand Jack, Lizzie."

Lizzie smiled. "Maybe I can be an animal behaviorist when I grow up." She had always figured she would be a vet, but maybe this would be an even more interesting way to help animals.

"I think you'd be terrific at that job, from what

your aunt tells me," said Eileen. "She says you have a way with dogs, and I can see that she's right."

"Maybe that's because I love them," said Lizzie.

"So do I." Eileen laughed. "That's why I enjoy my job so much. Come visit me at my office someday, and you can learn more about what I do."

Lizzie felt great when she got off the phone with Eileen. She *did* have a way with dogs. She knew just how to take care of them, train them, and most important, love them.

Before she went back outside, she went upstairs. "Did Kit Smithers write back yet?" she asked her mom after she'd told her all about Eileen's phone call.

"Not yet." Her mom frowned at her notes. "Remember, I said it might take a while."

When Lizzie went out the back door, she was surprised to see Charles and Buddy and the Bean running in circles around the backyard. She waved Charles down. "What are you doing?"

"Playing tag!" Charles bent over and panted. "The Bean is it!"

"But where's Jack?"

Charles looked over his shoulder. "I don't know. He was right behind me a second ago."

Jack was not in the rosebushes. He was not near the swing set. He was not behind the shed.

Jack was underneath the porch — and he was chewing on something.

"What have you got there, Jackie?" Lizzie asked. She had to get down on her hands and knees for a good view.

Then Lizzie's eyes adjusted to the dark and she saw what Jack was eating.

"*Mountain Girl!*" Her book! Her most beautiful, favorite book, all ripped to pieces.

CHAPTER EIGHT

Lizzie wanted to yell. She wanted to scream. But she bit her lip. It wasn't Jack's fault. It was hers. She never should have brought that book outside where he was playing. Jack looked up at her with his big shiny brown eyes. He had one paw on the book, and a slobbered-on shred of paper hung from his jaw.

Oops. Did I do something wrong again?

"No, Jack!" said Lizzie. "Leave it!" But the lump in her throat made it hard to talk. Plus she was so upset that she could hardly even remember what Eileen had said to do. Lizzie blinked back her tears.

"Lizzie!" Mom opened her study window and stuck out her head. "Lizzie, guess what? You just got a note back from Kit Smithers!"

Lizzie gasped. The ruined book forgotten, she ran inside and took the stairs two at a time, with Buddy and Jack scrabbling along behind her. "Let's see! What did she say? Did she answer my questions?"

Mom smiled as she let Lizzie sit down at her computer. "That was very nice of her, to write back so quickly. I'll go get myself a cup of coffee while you read. Maybe I should take Jack downstairs with me, too."

"Oh, let him stay!" said Lizzie. "He's good as long as someone's right there with him. I'll watch him." She barely noticed when her mother left the room. She was already reading Kit Smithers's letter.

Dear Lizzie,
    Thanks for your note! Fortunately, I just finished

my work for the day, so I have a chance to write back to you right away. I'm so glad you like my books. You're right, I do love dogs, but ☹ I don't have one right now. My old dog, Jasper, used to spend all day with me in my little writing cabin in the woods near my house. I miss his company, even though he snored!

As for your other questions:

I decided to be a writer because I love to write. It's the best job in the world, because I can work at home, even in my pajamas if I want.

I don't draw the pictures in my books, but I think the artist does a great job of bringing my characters to life, don't you?

My stories are sometimes *based* on true stories, but I make up a lot of the details. I plan to write many, many more books.

And finally, my favorite color is green. Maybe that's why I chose to live in the Green Mountain State.

Thanks again for writing, Lizzie. I liked the picture you sent. That must be Buddy in your lap, since he has a white spot in the shape of a heart on his chest. He's very cute. I bet your new foster puppy, Jack, is cute, too. My cousins had a boxer named Bailey, and I always loved that dog.

Your friend,

Kit Smithers

Lizzie sat back in her chair. "Wow!" It was so cool to get a letter back from someone as famous as Kit Smithers. She leaned forward and read the whole letter over again. Kit Smithers had answered every single question! Lizzie clicked "reply" and started writing.

Dear Kit Smithers,

Thanks for writing back to me! That is so cool. Wait till I tell my friend Maria!

I do like the pictures in your books and they do seem very real. I drew you a great picture of Sunny, from *Mountain Girl*, but Jack ate it. He eats everything. He even ate my *Mountain Girl* book. I know it is not really his fault. But I'm still kind of mad. And sad. That was my best book. Did your dog Jasper ever used to eat things?

Your best reader,

Lizzie Peterson

Lizzie clicked "send" just as her mom came back into the room. "Mom!" she said without turning around. "Kit Smithers wrote me the best letter! And I already wrote her back. She had a dog named Jasper. He snored, and —" Lizzie spun around in the chair. Why was Mom so quiet? And why did she look so mad? "Oh." Lizzie stopped talking when she saw what her mother was staring at.

Jack sat in the corner, munching quietly on a wad of paper. "Those are my notes!" Mom yelled. She ran over to Jack and grabbed the soggy, shredded mess out of his mouth. "No, Jack. No! Bad dog! Leave it!"

Jack looked up at her, wrinkling his forehead.

Oh, no! I messed up again.

Lizzie put her hands over her eyes. She could hardly bear to watch.

Mom plopped down on the floor and began to poke at the ruined notes. "I don't believe this," she muttered. "How am I ever going to write my article now?"

Lizzie felt awful. "It's all my fault!" She jumped up to help her mom. "I was supposed to be keeping an eye on Jack." She stared in dismay at the pile of pulp in her mother's hands. "I'm really sorry."

Mom sighed. "It's okay, Lizzie. I guess it's not the end of the world, any more than it was when he ate your letter." But she frowned down at Jack. "To tell you the truth, at this rate I'm not sure we'll even make it through two days with this puppy."

CHAPTER NINE

Lizzie stuck to Jack like glue for the rest of the day, making sure he did not put anything in his mouth that did not belong there. She played with him, worked on his sit pretty trick, gave him treats, and patted him.

At bedtime, Charles took Buddy into his room to sleep, and Dad helped Lizzie bring Jack's crate upstairs. She got the puppy all settled in, then climbed into her own bed. Jack was much quieter now that he wasn't all alone down in the kitchen. He whimpered a little bit at first, but when Lizzie told him to hush, he settled down with a sigh and soon he was snoring.

Nice for Jack — but Lizzie could not sleep a wink.

Jack sure was a handful. Where on earth was the perfect forever home for a dog who chewed and ate everything he could get his teeth into? It was only good luck that so far Jack had not eaten anything in the Petersons' house that would make him really sick. Mom and Dad would not be happy if they had to take him to the vet.

Lizzie knew she did not have long to find this puppy a home, but she was still sure she could do it — somehow. She believed that there was a perfect home for every puppy. She could not let Jack be the exception to that rule! She lay in bed and stared at the ceiling. She thought and thought. Jack needed attention all the time. Eileen had said that the perfect owner for Jack would live in the country and work at home. Lizzie knew that the person also had to be somebody who really loved dogs and would have the patience to train Jack. He was so smart. He could learn how to behave.

Suddenly, Lizzie sat straight up in bed. She

knew *just* the person! She looked at her clock. It was eleven-thirty at night — way too late to make a phone call. She would have to wait until morning. "I've got it, Jack!" She leaned over the bed to whisper to the snoozing pup. Then Lizzie lay back down and finally went to sleep.

Lizzie slept late the next morning, until almost ten o'clock. When she woke up, Jack's crate was empty. Lizzie couldn't believe it. How had he escaped? And how much trouble was he already in? Her heart pounded — until she spotted a little note attached to the crate's door. *Jack is downstairs*, it said in Dad's writing. Whew.

By the time she went down to breakfast, Dad was washing up the skillet he had used to make his famous blueberry pancakes. Charles and his friend Sammy (Sammy always showed up for blueberry pancakes) had finished eating and were playing on the floor with Jack and Buddy while the Bean sat at the table, singing a little song to himself as he finger-painted with the syrup that was left on his plate. "Good morning, sleepy-head!" Dad gave Lizzie a kiss on the top of her head. "Mom's already upstairs working. Want me to make you some pancakes?"

"That's okay." Lizzie wasn't thinking about breakfast. She was thinking about Jack's new home. "Guess what? I thought of the perfect forever home for Jack!"

Dad raised his eyebrows. "Really? That's great!"

"Who?" asked Charles.

"Mary Thompson! She's perfect. She works at home, she has a big yard, and she loves dogs. All the things Eileen said Jack needed," said Lizzie. "I'm going to call her."

"She won't take him." Charles went back to playing tug with Jack. "She already has two dogs."

Mary Thompson was a writer who had recently moved to Littleton. Lizzie had met her when Mary had adopted Cocoa and Cinnamon, Buddy's sisters. Now Mary had become a friend, and she and the Petersons got together regularly so the puppies could have a family reunion.

Lizzie stuck her tongue out at Charles. What did he know?

"Well," Dad said, "I suppose it might be worth a try. But why don't you give her another half hour or so before you call? People like to sleep late on weekends."

Lizzie didn't mind waiting. She was positive Mary would say yes, no matter what Charles said. She grabbed a piece of toast and headed upstairs. The door to Mom's study was closed. Lizzie knocked gently. "Mom? Did Kit Smithers write again?"

Mom looked tired. "Morning, sweetie. I'll check one more time. But I'm in a real pickle with this article, and I can't keep interrupting my work to look for your e-mail." Mom clicked a few keys and smiled. "Looks like there is something from her! Now that you and Kit are such friends, you can write to her from your own e-mail account. I'll forward it to you so you can read it on the other computer."

"Thanks, Mom!" Lizzie ran down the hall and sat at the computer.

Dear Lizzie,

What a shame that Jack ate your copy of *Mountain Girl*. (If I was a stuck-up writer, I might say he had good taste!) My dog Jasper used to eat things all the time when he was a puppy. He was a black Lab, and they are famous for eating things. Once Jasper ate a box of rubber bands! But he learned, and I bet Jack will, too. Can you send me a picture of Jack? I'm dying to see what he looks like.

Your friend,

Kit Smithers

Lizzie smiled as she read the letter. Then she wrote back quickly.

Dear Kit Smithers,

Too bad you live in Texas, so far away. Otherwise you could adopt Jack. See how cute he is? But I think I might have found him a home. Wish me luck!

Your friend,

Lizzie Peterson

She attached three of the cutest pictures she had taken of Jack, sent the e-mail, then went back downstairs to call Mary Thompson.

"Hi, Mary! It's Lizzie." Lizzie raced through her hellos and asked about Mary's puppies. Then she told Mary all about Jack. Well, maybe not *all* about him. She left out some of the truth about his strange eating habits. "He'll be the perfect addition to your family!" she finished. "When can we bring him over?"

"Oh, Lizzie." Mary sighed. "I would love to help you, but I can't possibly take on another dog."

CHAPTER TEN

"You know that I adore Cocoa and Cinnamon," Mary went on, "but the two of them keep me plenty busy. Some days I can barely get any writing done, and my house is in a state."

Lizzie's face fell.

Charles and Sammy came in from outside just then, with Jack and Buddy tumbling after them. Charles gave Lizzie a questioning look, and Lizzie shook her head sadly. Charles was right: Mary was not going to adopt Jack. After Lizzie hung up, she waited to hear Charles say "I told you so." But he just shrugged and gave her a superior little smile, which was even more annoying.

Lizzie sat on the kitchen floor and pulled Jack close for a hug. "You've been a good boy," she said, "even though I know it's only because we have been watching you every minute. And we can't do that forever. I just know the perfect home is out there, waiting for you." She kissed his adorable wrinkly forehead. "Mary said her house is in a state," she informed Charles. "Whatever that means. Like what, the Green Mountain State?" She remembered what Kit Smithers had written.

"Vermont!" Charles said.

"Vermont?" Lizzie stared at him. "What do you mean, Vermont? The Green Mountain State has got to be Texas. That's where Kit Smithers lives." Lizzie tried to remember what she'd learned about the states last year. How could Charles possibly know more than she did when he was only in second grade?

Charles shook his head. "I saw it on a sign when we went to Vermont last winter. 'Welcome to Vermont, the Green Mountain State.'"

"Charles is absolutely right," said Dad, who had come into the kitchen from the garage, where he was changing the oil in his pickup truck. He wiped his hands on a rag. "The name Vermont comes from the French words for green, *vert*, and mountain, *mont*. Vermont was the fourteenth state to join the Union, and —"

Dad had a habit of sometimes telling you more than you wanted to know. But Lizzie had stopped listening. She gave Jack one more kiss on the head, moved him off her lap, and pounded up the stairs. She had to write to Kit Smithers right away.

But when Lizzie checked her e-mail, she got a big surprise. There was a note waiting for her!

Dear Lizzie,

I'm glad to hear that you may have found Jack a home — but to tell you the truth, I'm sorry, too. I was just about to ask you if I could adopt him! I think Jack would fit in perfectly with my country life. (I don't live in Texas anymore, by the way. I moved to Vermont last year.) But the important thing is that he has found a good home. Please let me know if anything changes. Good luck with your puppy fostering!

Your friend,

Kit Smithers

Underneath her name, Kit Smithers had put her phone number. Lizzie's hands flew as she typed a quick answer and wrote down the phone number on a scrap of paper. Then she ran downstairs and out into the garage. "Dad! Dad! Can we go to Vermont? Maybe today?"

Dad stared at her from under the open hood of his truck. "What?"

Lizzie gave him the scrap of paper with Kit Smithers's phone number on it. "Kit Smithers wants to adopt Jack. Will you call her and find out how long it would take to get to where she lives? Please? Please?"

Dad frowned down at the number. "It seems crazy," he said. "But we do need to find Jack a home before he eats our whole house. And your mom could definitely use some peace and quiet so she can finish up her article." He wiped his hands on a rag and slammed the hood. Lizzie followed him into the kitchen and stuck right by him while he called the number on the paper and started talking. She couldn't believe that her dad was actually speaking to *the* Kit Smithers!

Finally, he hung up and turned to Lizzie with a big grin. "Okay, we're on! She still wants Jack and it'll only take a couple of hours to get there. We can pile everybody in the van right after lunch."

"Pile everybody in the van? Where are you going?" Mom bounced into the kitchen, looking much more cheerful than she had in days. "Guess what?" she asked without waiting for an answer to her first question. "It turns out Jack brought me some good luck. Since I couldn't read those notes he chewed, I finally had to call the builder again. We had the best conversation!"

Dad and Lizzie looked at each other. But Mom

just kept rattling on as she moved from fridge to counter, making herself a sandwich.

"It turns out he has two boxers, so he knew exactly what we are dealing with here. Anyway, we talked for a while and suddenly I understood everything so much better! All I have to do now is write it all down." She picked up the plate with her sandwich on it, ready to go back to her computer. "I asked the guy if he wanted another boxer, but he turned me down. But that's okay. Now that Jack is my lucky puppy, I don't mind if we keep him a little longer."

"Uh, Mom?" Lizzie had been waving a hand at her mother for a while. "News flash! We found a home for Jack!"

Mom put down her plate. "Really?"

"Really," said Lizzie. And she told her mom the whole story.

An hour later, Dad pulled the van out of the Petersons' driveway. Lizzie sat next to the Bean, who was dozing in his car seat. Charles and Sammy sat behind them, and Jack was in his crate in the very back. Buddy was staying home to keep Mom company.

"Knock, knock," Sammy said before they'd even turned the corner.

Lizzie groaned. Was she going to have to listen to Sammy and her brother tell terrible jokes for the next two hours? She closed her eyes and pictured what it would be like to meet Kit Smithers. She had so many things to ask her about, and to tell her. Lizzie wanted to know when Kit had written her first book, and whether she had any brothers or sisters. She wanted to tell Kit about the horse story she and Maria planned to write together, about an Arabian colt who runs away from its cruel owner. And she definitely wanted to explain all about Jack and how to take care of him. Lizzie and Kit Smithers were going to have a lot to talk about.

As they drove north, Lizzie watched the scenery change. Soon there were fewer stores and houses, and more fields and forests. Lizzie loved driving north. It reminded her of her family's winter vacation to Vermont, where she had met and fostered Bear, the cutest, smartest husky puppy in the world. Sometimes Lizzie still wished she could have kept Bear for herself, but she knew he was happy in his new home — just like Jack was going to be.

Finally, Dad turned down a bumpy, rutted dirt road with trees on either side, then drove up a long driveway to a log cabin that sat high on a hill, surrounded by tall trees. There was a smaller cabin next to it. Lizzie spotted a tall, lanky person chopping wood outside the smaller cabin. When the person looked up, Lizzie realized that it was Kit Smithers. She put down her ax and waved, smiling broadly as everyone piled out of the van. "Welcome, welcome!" she said. She looked straight at Lizzie. "Hello, Lizzie. I'd know that face anywhere."

Lizzie tried to say something, but no words came out. Her face felt hot. She ducked her head. She could not seem to say a single thing! She felt like jumping back in the van. Was this what it was like to be shy? Lizzie had never felt that way before. It was horrible!

But Kit Smithers smiled around at everyone as Dad introduced himself, the Bean, Charles, and Sammy. "And here's the guest of honor." He opened up the back of the van to show Jack sitting up, all perky and happy in his crate.

"Jack!" Kit Smithers unlatched the door of the crate and helped Jack jump out. "Welcome home, Jack!" She knelt down and opened her arms wide.

With a jingle of tags, Jack shook himself, wriggling happily as he pranced over to lick Kit's chin.

Hello! I don't know who you are, but I love you already!

"He's beautiful," Kit said. "And once he's used to the place, he can run around to his heart's content. There are no other houses for miles, and plenty of room to roam. Or he can just snooze on the floor next to me while I write in my cabin. We're going to be very happy together, aren't we, Jack?"

Lizzie and Charles smiled at each other. Suddenly, she didn't feel annoyed by him anymore, not one bit. So what if he had been right about her letter? And about Mary Thompson. And, okay, also about Vermont being the Green Mountain State. Lizzie had also been right about something: that she could find the perfect home for Jack.

Eventually, Lizzie got over her shyness enough to tell Kit Smithers all about how to take care of Jack. By the time they left, Lizzie was pretty sure that Kit was going to love the little boxer pup and that he would love his new forever home. But she didn't feel absolutely, positively sure that everything was settled until the following Friday. That day, when Lizzie came home from school, she found a package addressed to her waiting on the hall table. It was from Kit Smithers! She tore open the wrapping and found a book: a brand-new hardcover copy of *Mountain Girl*, just as beautiful as the one Jack had chewed up. Best of all, when she opened it up to the title page, she saw that Kit had signed it.

For Lizzie, who brought Jack into my life.
With many thanks, Kit Smithers

Puppy Tips

Some puppies and dogs will eat just about anything. Everything Jack ate in this book was eaten by a puppy or dog in real life — and I still have a list about two pages long of *other* things that dogs have eaten, including TV remotes, whole turkeys, and earrings. Funny? Sort of. But dogs can get very sick or even die from eating the wrong things. (Besides chocolate, did you know grapes, raisins, and onions can also make dogs sick?) It's important to make sure your puppy doesn't have the chance to eat things that are bad for him. Keep him in his crate whenever you can't keep an eye on him, and teach him the "leave it" command. If your puppy has eaten something strange and is throwing up or having diarrhea, he may need to go to the vet. Most puppies grow out of the chewing stage, but if yours doesn't you might have to consult an animal behaviorist or dog trainer for more help.

Dear Reader,

My dogs Jack and Molly once ate a whole *bookshelf's* worth of books. My dog Junior ate a beautiful loaf of Italian bread I had just baked. My aunt Jo's dog Chester ate a poisonous mushroom. And Django ate all kinds of things: a corner of a rug, some mail, a whole tray of burritos, and a yucky dead animal. Django got very, very sick one time from something he had eaten (I'm not even sure what it was). He had to spend the night at the vet's and I was so worried. It can be very hard to teach dogs — especially Labs! — not to eat things they shouldn't.

Yours from the Puppy Place,
Ellen Miles

P.S. If you loved Jack's crazy eating habits, check out the messes that a pesky pug named Pugsley makes in this funny Puppy Place book:

Charles smiled down at Sweetie, the apricot-colored miniature poodle puppy the Petersons had just agreed to foster. The tiny, curly-haired puppy stared back at Charles with the brightest black eyes he had ever seen. Her coat was springy and soft. She felt delicate, like a fancy piece of china that might break if you even *looked* at it the wrong way. "We'll take care of you," he promised. He turned to Lizzie. "Where's Buddy? Let's see if they get along."

"I put him in my bedroom until Sweetie got comfortable here," said Lizzie. She went to get Buddy, and Charles and the Bean took Sweetie into the living room to play. Charles put the little puppy down on the rug and watched as she ran around sniffing everything. She tried to pick up one of Buddy's stuffed toys, but it was almost bigger than she was! Sweetie tugged and growled, trying to pull Mr. Duck out of the toy basket.

Just then, Lizzie ran back downstairs with Buddy trotting after her.

"Uh-oh," said Charles. Mr. Duck was one of Buddy's favorite toys. Maybe he wouldn't be so happy to find another puppy playing with it.

But Buddy ran right over to Sweetie, wagging his tail. He pulled Mr. Duck out of the basket and laid him down in front of Sweetie.

Here you go!

Buddy bowed down, his front paws stretched way out in front.

Want to play?

Sweetie bowed back — and they were off, racing around the room. After a few laps, Buddy rolled over and let Sweetie climb on him.

"Wow!" said Charles. "Everybody loves Sweetie."

"Evvybody love Sweetie!" echoed the Bean. He laughed his googly laugh. "The Bean love Sweetie, Charles love Sweetie, Lizzie love Sweetie, Buddy love Sweetie! Dada and Mama love Sweetie!"

Sweetie looked up, one tiny foot planted on Buddy's chest, and cocked her head.

Of course! And I love you all, too!

Charles laughed. Sweetie was so cute. "Up, Sweetie!" he said, patting his knee. Sweetie ran over and jumped, sailing through the air like a little ball of fluff. She landed perfectly on Charles's lap. "Good girl!" He gave her a big kiss on the top of her head.

That's when Buddy started to bark.

ABOUT THE AUTHOR

Ellen Miles likes to write about the different personalities of dogs. She is the author of more than 28 books, including the Puppy Place and Taylor-Made Tales series as well as *The Pied Piper* and other Scholastic Classics. Ellen loves to be outdoors every day, walking, biking, skiing, or swimming, depending on the season. She also loves to read, cook, explore her beautiful state, and hang out with friends and family. She lives in Vermont.

If you love animals, be sure to read all the adorable stories in the Puppy Place series!

Cat Magic

Lottie spends the summer in her uncle's pet shop. She loves talking to the animals. But what happens when the animals start to talk back?

Dog Magic

What has four legs, a French accent, and magical powers? A dachshund named Sophie! She and her owner live in a very special pet shop where magic is in the air and the animals have a lot to say.

Hamster Magic

Lottie's best friend is acting strangely. Luckily, a new hamster, Giles, arrives just in time to help her.